## The Playground in the Morning Before School [Malcolm]

Soft morning
sun shining
brand-new day
and the playground mine
except for the lady who comes
with her black bag
her stick with a nail on the end
picking up trash
making the playground nice

Just her
just me
at the top of the monkey bars
looking across the bay
to the city on the other side
the pointy building like a witch's hat
that round tower on the hill
I pretend I can see the Golden Gate Bridge.

FARRAR STRAUS GIROUX • NEW YORK

# SPEAK TO ME

## (AND I WILL LISTEN BETWEEN THE LINES)

Karen English • Pictures by Amy June Bates

## I Gave My Teacher a Flower [Lamont]

I gave my teacher a flower
On Monday
She smiled at me—
"Thank you, Lamont"
—Then put it in water
In a jar on her desk
Where I could see it
First thing
Walking through the door
Tuesday, Wednesday, Thursday
And be happy
That I could do something so wonderful
To give my teacher a flower
Even when
Today (Friday)
I see my flower
Head down on its stem
Sad-like
And time to be gone
So I can give my teacher a new flower
And we can both be happy all over again.

## I Don't Care [Tyrell]

I just got here and
Already I don't care about anything this day
Send me next door to Miss Cross's room
And I don't care
Bench me for recess
And I don't care
Make me write: "I'll do my work quietly"
One hundred times
And I don't care
I don't care about anything this day
And you can't make me.

## THE READING BOY [MALCOLM]

Omar came on Monday
We liked him quick because he can read
As good as the teacher

Tyrell looked at him long and hard
As the river of words flowed out of his mouth
On one breath
The reading boy

Lamont asked to change his seat
To the one by the reading boy
Who sang the words off the page

Teacher asked him a question
And everyone listened
He is the one who reads.

## EIGHT [RICA]

Eight
I'm eight today
In third grade
Curving my letters
Swirling them where I want
Combing Neecy's hair into squares
'Cause I know how to make a straight part
A twist on each square
And a barrette on each twist
In red
Or blue
Or pink
(Me and Brianna and Neecy
Love pink so much
We have a pink-lovers club called
We Love Pink!)
Mama letting me cook
'Cause my hands are getting bigger
Getting to be a hall monitor
With a sky-blue jacket
That rustles
Telling all the second graders
Hush!
Walk!
Fishing with Paw-Paw
'Cause I'll know how to be quiet

Going to the store
With money and a list
That I can read
Counting money into Miss Johnson's hand
Getting it right
Eight is sweet
Eight is pretty
Eight is bigger than my cousin Mookie being seven
I like the way it looks
One doughnut on top of another
A figure eight on ice
Good and happy and strong

Somebody someday soon will ask me:
Rica, how old are you?
And I'll get to say: Eight!

## Got Me a New Baby Brother [Neecy]

Hey Rica
I got me a new baby brother
And he looks like me
My grandma said
He's got my hair
My big forehead
My hands
My fingers
My long nose
I love my new baby brother
Because he looks just like me.

### I'll Be Your Best Friend [Brianna]

I'll be your best friend, Neecy
Walk you to the restroom
Comb your hair the way you want
Give you my chips
Sneak you sunflower seeds under the desk
Share my new pink eraser
Be a turner when you're the jumper
Hold my umbrella more over your head than mine
Paint your nails
Let you use my markers
My cherry lip gloss
I'll be your best friend again and hold your hand
Sit next to you in the cafeteria
Take up for you.

## PINK INK [RICA]

My teacher said no pink ink
When I've been waiting all morning
to use my new pink ink
Teacher said
Journals out
Write about yesterday

I thought
I'll write about yesterday
In pink ink
How nice my words will look
In the pink ink of my new pink-ink pen
But she said: NO PINK INK
Use a pencil, Rica.

## I'm Tellin' [Lamont]

I'm tellin'
I'm tellin' now
No escape from my tattletellin'
No reprieve
No change of heart
When I'm set to tell
My tongue itching
My words ready
I'm growing a loud voice
Rising from my seat
Marching up to Teacher
Taking a deep breath
And tellin' what you did.

## TEACHER SAID [TYRELL]

Teacher said:
Don't be an excuse-maker
If you make excuses now
You'll make excuses all the rest of your life
And people will say,
"Here comes the ol' excuse-maker . . ."
Your boss will fire you
Your friends will leave you
Your children will shake their heads
Every time you open your mouth
An excuse will fall out
Excuse-making
Just a bad habit—that's all that is.

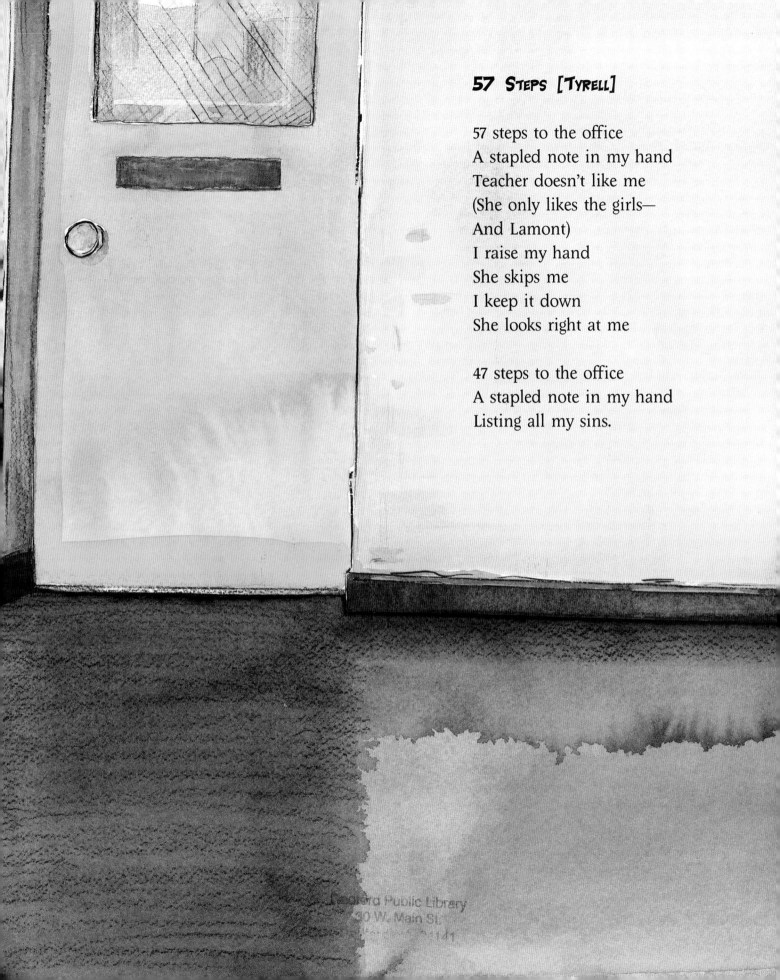

## 57 Steps [Tyrell]

57 steps to the office
A stapled note in my hand
Teacher doesn't like me
(She only likes the girls—
And Lamont)
I raise my hand
She skips me
I keep it down
She looks right at me

47 steps to the office
A stapled note in my hand
Listing all my sins.

## DAYDREAM [MALCOLM]

Yesterday we saw a film about water
The open sea
Boats with white sails
I'd like to be in a boat like that on blue water
Wind in the sails
Whoosh and I'd be gone
Today we saw a film about clouds
Long loose clouds
Tall fluffy ones
Clouds that spread like spilled milk
Across the wide sky
I'd like to be on a cloud
Way up high
Far away from here.

## What I Like about Neecy [Rica]

Her color richer than mine
Her eyes with thick lashes
Her laugh like a waterfall
Her learning dances fast
And teaching them to me
Her skating backwards at the roller rink
Her showing me new things to eat
Salt on lemons
Peppermint sticks in a pickle
Licking Kool-Aid out my palm
Eating kumquats from the neighbor's tree
Riding a bike with no hands
Steering with her knees
Painting my nails
Combing my hair
Knowing the words to the song
Faster than anyone.

### CAN YOU DO THIS? [NEECY]

Hey, Rica . . .
Can you do this?
Can you lean across the line
And sock the tetherball
From my side?
Like I can from your side?
Can you stoop and turn under the jump rope?
Can you run through it?
Can you dance?
I mean really dance?

## MY SPOT [LAMONT]

This is my spot . . .
My spot!
I put my jacket on it
I *saved* it
I *claimed* it
My spot
In the whole wide world
At this moment

You can't just cut me
Out of my spot
My marked spot
My branded spot
My *my* spot
You can't shove me
Out of the way
Make like I'm not here

I staked this spot
I put my jacket on this spot
To be first in line
I made it mine.

## No Saving Seats [Brianna]

No saving seats, Neecy
No saving a seat in the cafeteria for Rica
No stretching your leg across the bench
Or fanning out your elbows on the table
Yelling out to everyone: You can't sit here!
'Cause now you and Rica are best friends
When you were best friends with me yesterday

And no switching lunches
No changing your corn dog
For her pizza
'Cause you should know what you want
Beforehand
Before you get to the cafeteria lady

And no whispering in each other's ears or giggling
'Cause you talkin' with your mouth full
And showing chewed-up food
And making people around you feel bad
Real bad.

### I Got Two Jellybeans [Lamont]

I got two jellybeans
For staying in line
Doing my part
Keeping the line straight
Walking not running
Arms at my side
Head forward
Not lagging
Coming to a quick stop
When the line leader checked to see if we were
Straight
Head forward
Arms at our sides
Walking
Not running
Today I got two green jellybeans
For doing my part.

## I'M GOING TO LOUISIANA WHERE IT SNOWS [TYRELL]

I'm going to Louisiana where it snows
Not coming back to this school no more
Me and my grandmother
Moving to Louisiana
And getting us a house
With a yard
And a blue velvet couch
And my own bedroom
For just me
And my own TV
A kitchen with a table in it
And a window
So when I eat my cereal
I can look out that window
And see snow in Louisiana.

## No Such Thing as a Red Cake [Brianna]

There's no such thing as a red cake
Neecy says over my shoulder
(Like she should know)
"There's no such thing as a red cake, Brianna"
When I was liking the cake I was painting
Making my cake big and the people small
So there would be plenty
For some left over

"That cake's too big and those people are too small"
(Like she should know)
"And there's no such thing as a red cake"

I tell Neecy
"There is if I want there to be"
I paint everything the way I want it.

## My Real Daddy [Rica]

My real daddy's coming for me after school
To buy me whatever I want
To take me in his arms
Drive me all around
Show me off
Whisper secrets in my ear
Announce to everyone
"This is my princess!"
My real daddy's coming
To love me more than anyone or anything
No matter what.

## I Come from the Ones Who Lived [Malcolm]

My teacher told me something today
She said
I come from the ones who lived
I come from the ones who made the long journey
From a faraway place
And lived
I come from the ones who left mommies and daddies
Sisters and brothers
Everyone and everything
And lived
I come from the ones chained in dark, scary places
In hot, choking air
Starved, beaten
Terrified and alone
Torn from their homes
But lived
I come from the ones who knew they would not
Could not live
Yet still lived.

## FIVE MORE MINUTES AND I'LL GET TO GO HOME [TYRELL]

Five more minutes and I'll get to go home
What else is there to say?

## WALKING HOME MAKES ME FEEL GOOD [TYRELL]

Walking home makes me feel good
I can take my time
If I want to
Run
If I want to
Call out to Malcolm walking with some other kids
If I want to
Join up with them

I can stop at the corner store
Spend my quarter
Talk to Mr. Song
About whatever I want

Or—I can go another way
Down Adeline Street
Through the park
Next to the basketball court
Shoot some hoops
If there's a game going on
And they let me
Run down the grassy hill
And turn a flip I been practicing
If I want to

I can do anything I want
If I want to
Because it's after school
And I'm free!

## So Long a Day [Malcolm]

So long a day it was
Early morning was a brush of crimson in the sky
Early morning was shrugging into my school clothes
Keeping my eyes shut against being all the way awake
Stumbling into the kitchen
Where all was quiet
Except
The kitchen clock clicking minutes
Until it was hurry, hurry
Grab things, forget things
Loop back through the rooms
And out the door down to the bus stop
With Mama
And Baby Champ in the stroller
Bus bumping and lurching all the way to school
"Pull the cord, Malcolm"
Mama said to me
She got off, waved goodbye
Champ to the sitter
Mama to work

So long a day it was
Spelling test and times tables and topic sentences
Through recess and fish sticks at lunch
And a long list of what I need
For a book report due next Friday

So long a day it was
And the best part was
Getting to the playground
When it was empty and quiet
(Except the lady cleaning it up)
And me thinking
This is mine
All mine

And now I wait for Mama
And Baby Champ
And the bus.

For all the children whose words I've heard
by listening between the lines
—K.E.

For all teachers who listen
between the lines
—A.J.B.

THAT'S WORD [MALCOLM]

THAT'S WORD
A TRUER THING NEVER SAID
AND EVERYBODY KNOWS IT.

MAR  3 2005

www.fsgkidsbooks.com

Library of Congress Cataloging-in-Publication Data
English, Karen.
    Speak to me / Karen English ; pictures by Amy June Bates.
        p.   cm.
    Summary: Describes events of one day at a San Francisco Bay Area school as perceived by different third-graders, from the observations of first to arrive on the playground to the walk home.
    ISBN 0-374-37156-3
    [1. Schools—Fiction.   2. San Francisco (Calif.)—Fiction.]   I. Bates, Amy June, ill.   II. Title.

PZ7.E7232Sr 2004
[E]—dc21

                                        2002192895